All children face many new experiences as they grow up, and helping them to understand and deal with each is one of the most demanding and rewarding things we do as parents. Helping Hand Books are for both children and parents to read, perhaps together. Each simple story describes a childhood experience and shows some of the ways in which to make it a positive one. I do hope these books encourage children and parents to talk about these sometimes difficult issues. Talking together goes a long way to finding a solution.

Sarah

Sarah, Duchess of York

Ashley was bored.

She had been following her mommy around a store all afternoon. And now Mommy had met a friend and they were having a long talk about shopping, the weather, and a TV show they had seen the night before.

Ashley
Learns
About
Strangers

By Sarah, Duchess of York

Illustrated by Ian Cunliffe

STERLING

New York / London

STERLING and the distinctive Sterling logo are registered trademarks of
Sterling Publishing Co., Inc.

Library of Congress Cataloging-in-Publication Data

York, Sarah Mountbatten-Windsor, Duchess of, 1959-
[Daisy learns about strangers]
Ashley learns about strangers / by Sarah, Duchess of York ; illustrated by Ian Cunliffe.
p. cm. -- (Helping hand)
Summary: When Ashley wanders away from her mother while they are shopping and then
cannot find her, she approaches a security guard and is soon reunited with her mother.
Includes note to parents.
ISBN 978-1-4027-7393-8
[1. Strangers--Fiction. 2. Safety--Fiction. 3. Schools--Fiction.] I. Cunliffe, Ian, ill. II. Title.
PZ7.Y823As 2010
[E]--dc22

2009042148

Lot #:
2 4 6 8 10 9 7 5 3 1
04/10
Published by Sterling Publishing Co., Inc.
387 Park Avenue South, New York, NY 10016
Story and illustrations © 2007 by Startworks Ltd
'Ten Helpful Hints' © 2009 by Startworks Ltd
Distributed in Canada by Sterling Publishing
c/o Canadian Manda Group, 165 Dufferin Street
Toronto, Ontario, Canada M6K 3H6
Distributed in Australia by Capricorn Link (Australia) Pty. Ltd.
P.O. Box 704, Windsor, NSW 2756, Australia

Sterling ISBN 978-1-4027-7393-8

For information about custom editions, special sales, premium and
corporate purchases, please contact Sterling Special Sales
Department at 800-805-5489 or specialsales@sterlingpublishing.com.

Ashley noticed a wall of TVs in another corner of the store. There was a cartoon showing. It was much more interesting than listening to Mommy and her friend.

Ashley wandered away.

As she got closer to the TVs, she could hear music and voices. Soon she was completely lost in what she was watching and forgot all about her mommy . . .

. . . who had not noticed Ashley walking away.

Ashley was nowhere to be seen.

Her mommy gripped her friend's arm in panic, looking around in every direction.

Meanwhile the cartoon was over and Ashley suddenly realized where she was. Or rather where she wasn't.

She wasn't with her mommy anymore. As she looked around at all the people walking past her, she felt very alone.

Then Ashley remembered what she had been told to do if she ever got lost. She looked for someone in a uniform.

There was a man near the front of the store wearing a uniform with the word "Security" on it. Ashley rushed up to him and said, "Excuse me, but I've lost my mommy. She was near the carrots, but I walked away and now she's gone and I don't know if I'll ever see her again."

Ashley's lip began to tremble. She wanted to cry, but she tried hard not to.

The security guard knelt down and said to Ashley, "Don't worry. I'm sure she didn't go very far. Tell me your name and we'll find her."

Soon there was an announcement over the store loudspeaker:

"Will the mother of Ashley Johnson please come to the manager's office?"

Ashley's mommy was in the manager's office before you could say Ashley Johnson!

"Why did you wander off, Ashley?" asked her mommy. "You know you must stay with me when we are out shopping."

Ashley could see that her mommy had been crying, and now she couldn't stop herself either. She gave her mommy the biggest hug.

The manager didn't like seeing Ashley cry, so he explained to her that she had done the right thing in going to a security guard.

"You were very smart to find someone in a uniform to help you, Ashley," he said.

That night Ashley's mommy and daddy explained that a stranger is someone you don't know and who has not been introduced to you by an adult you trust. They also told Ashley that even though most grown-ups are nice to children, there are some who are not nice, even if at first they may seem to be.

"So it's important to remember a few simple rules if you happen to be approached by a grown-up you don't know," said her daddy. "Let's make up a rhyme so the rules are easy to remember."

They found a piece of paper and wrote:

Don't be alone, wherever you go.
You'll be much safer with people you know.
Don't take a stranger's candy or treat
or talk to strangers you might meet.
Strangers may not be as nice as they seem,
so if you get scared, it's okay to scream.
And never get into a stranger's car.
Stick with these rules wherever you are.

The next day, Ashley showed her rhyme to Mrs. Matthews, her teacher. She asked Ashley to read it to the rest of the class.

When she was finished, Mrs. Matthews asked the class if they had any questions about strangers. Ethan put up his hand.

"Is it okay to talk to a stranger if they say they know my mom and dad?" asked Ethan.

"That's a very good question," said Mrs. Matthews. "If a stranger tells you they know your parents, but you don't know them, they are still a stranger to you. Always check first with an adult you trust, and never go off with someone you don't know, no matter what they tell you."

"Let's all say Ashley's rhyme one more time," said Mrs. Matthews.

So they did.

Don't be alone, wherever you go.
You'll be much safer with people you know.
Don't take a stranger's candy or treat
or talk to strangers you might meet.
Strangers may not be as nice as they seem,
so if you get scared, it's okay to scream.
And never get into a stranger's car.
Stick with these rules wherever you are.

And when the children met their parents that afternoon to go home, they all knew the rules that would make them safe.

TEN HELPFUL HINTS
FOR PARENTS WARNING THEIR CHILDREN ABOUT STRANGERS

By Dr. Richard Woolfson, PhD

1. Explain that appearances can be deceptive. Your child can't always tell who is a "bad stranger" just by looking at them. Make it clear that a stranger could appear friendly, generous, and caring, even if they are not. Try to explain this clearly to avoid confusion. It's important for your child to be careful, but she shouldn't think that all people are actually dangerous.

2. Be clear but practical. For instance, there is no point in telling your child "Don't talk to strangers when you are away from home" because that would not be possible. It would mean he couldn't talk to police officers or to people who might be at a friend's house while he is there, and so on.

3. Make it absolutely clear, though, that your child should never, ever walk away with a stranger or out of a store with them or go into a vehicle with them, no matter what that person says to them.

4. Present practical examples. Tell your child, for example, "Don't take the hand of someone you don't know when you are in the street or in the park" or "Never take candy from someone you don't know when you are not in our home" or "Never get into a car with a person you do not know." The more specific the examples, the better.

5. Give these reminders regularly. Young children forget instructions from parents quickly, so get into the habit of reminding your child about stranger danger each time she goes out, especially as her independence increases.

6. Let your child ask as many questions as he wants. His curiosity is endless and the whole concept of stranger danger is complicated. Allow him to ask any questions he wants about this without making him feel that he is being a bother.

7. Emphasize to your child that nobody has a right to touch her unless she is comfortable with that touch. She will understand that a hug from you is perfectly acceptable but that it is not okay when it comes from someone she doesn't know (assuming you are not with her).

8. Tell your child what to do if he gets lost. Instruct him to ask for help from someone in a uniform, and if he doesn't know what a uniform is, show him pictures of, say, a police officer or security guard. Explain to your child that if there is no one in a uniform around, he should find someone in a position of trust, such as a teacher or parent with children.

9. Don't take anything for granted and always keep a close eye on your child in public. It only takes a second for your child to slip out of your line of vision. For instance, she might absently wander off while you chat to a store assistant or talk on your cell phone.

10. Tailor your comments to your child's age. He may ask, "What will happen to me if I go with a stranger?" Instead of terrifying him, give a basic explanation, such as "A stranger might hurt you." This provides a sufficient degree of warning with out making the emotional impact of the message too extreme.

Dr. Richard Woolfson is a child psychologist, working with children and their families. He is also an author and has written several books on child development and family life, in addition to numerous articles for magazines and newspapers. Dr. Woolfson runs training workshops for parents and child care professionals and appears regularly on radio and television. He is a Fellow of the British Psychological Society.

Helping Hand Books

Look for these other helpful books to share with your child:

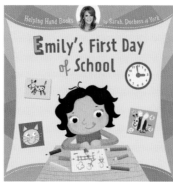